Published in Australia by Truebridges Media

First published in Australia 2021
Copyright © Niels van Hove 2021
All rights reserved. No part of this publication may be reproduced, stored in a retrieval system, or transmitted, in any form or by any means without the prior written permission of the publisher, nor be otherwise circulated in any form of binding or cover other than that in which it is published and without a similar condition being imposed on the subsequent purchaser.

National Library of Australia Cataloguing-in-Publication entry
Creator: Van Hove, Niels
Title: My Strong Mind IV: I am Pro-active and Keep my Emotions in Check
ISBN: 978-0-6452336-1-2 (ebook)
ISBN: 978-0-6452336-0-5 (Paperback - KDP)
ISBN: 978-0-6452336-3-6 (Hardback - Ingramspark)
ISBN: 978-0-6452336-2-9 (Paperback - Ingramspark)

Target Audience: For primary school age
Subjects: Juvenile fiction. Confidence in children. Self-esteem. Toughness (personal trait).

Cover layout and illustrations by Vanlaldiki
Typesetting by Nelly Murariu (PixBeeDesign.com)
Printed by Kindle Direct Publishing & Ingramspark

Disclaimer
All care has been taken in the preparation of the information herein, but no responsibility can be accepted by the publisher or author for any damages resulting from the misinterpretation of this work. All contact details given in this book were current at the time of publication, but are subject to change.

Jack and Kate are **good friends**.
They enjoy learning and playing together.

When they walk home from school,
they often talk about **improving**
their **strong** mind.

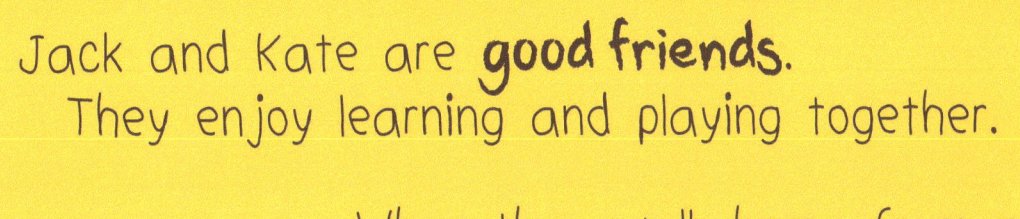

The 4 C's of My Strong Mind

Commitment: I set goals and work hard to deliver them
Control: I'm pro-active and keep my emotions in check
Challenge: I stretch myself and learn from everything
Confidence: I have the ability and can stand my ground

At school, their teacher taught them that you can use your **strong mind** to improve **control**.

Control means that you:

- can choose how you **react** to any situation.
- you believe you have the **power** to make **positive** change.
- you take **action** by yourself.

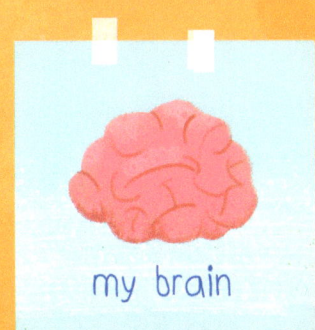

Kate and Jack realised that being in **control** is not always **easy**.

- It is hard to **stay calm** when something bad happens to you.
- Some situations feel like they are too **overwhelming** to do something about.
- There are things that you really **cannot** control.

They wanted to share **everything** they **learned** just with you!

Sometimes I get really **nervous**.
Like when I have to do Show and Tell in front of the class.

Or when I have to play an **important** basketball game.

Luckily, I learned **some tricks** to calm my mind.

I can take five big breaths: 1...2...3...4...

Controlling my breath helps me control my emotions.

I can do things like colouring in, a puzzle, or an origami.

5...

Mindful exercises distract my mind and control my nerves.

Sometimes boys are **mean**. They make fun of me or call me names. That can make me very, very **angry**.

I can **count to 10 to calm** myself down.

I learned that if you cannot control something, it is better not to worry too much about it.

That worrying is just a waste of your energy.

I love to **play** my favourite **game** on the iPad.

My mum says,

'Kate, you can **control your screentime**. Or how much you help your mother.

'So, stop playing on the iPad and help me set the table please.'

I can get very upset when I can't find a toy or my soccer ball.

Then my mum asks,

'How big is your problem, Jack?'

EMOTIONAL ZONE

GREEN	AMBER	RED

Feeling: Good, happy	Feeling: Frustrated	Feeling: Angry, anxious

Together we then check my **emotional zone.**

Understanding my emotional zone helps me **handle my problem.**

One day my father and I went to the shop.

He put on a large sombrero and said,
'Let's put a smile on people's faces.'

I put on a funny wig. Everyone in the shop laughed. My dad and I chose to try and make people laugh.

And it worked!

Jack and I wanted to **do some good for other people.**

We decided to play games in a nursing home.

Those grannies were lonely and loved to play games with us.

We chose to be kind and **made** a little **difference** in someone's life.

Kate and Jack try to make a positive difference and choose how to react to any situation.

This is how they improve their control.

Showing control can be hard, but Jack and Kate do not easily give up.

Every time they try, their **minds grow** just a little bit **stronger.**

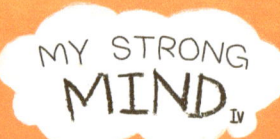

Control

My name is _____
and I am pro-active and keep my emotions in check.

Unexpected events I don't like
_____
_____

How can I react?
_____
_____

How do they make me feel?
_____
_____

My emotional zone

4. I'm really mad.

3. I'm getting frustrated.

2. I feel a little upset.

1. I feel good.

What can I do?

_____
_____

_____
_____

_____
_____

_____
_____

Problems I can control	Problems I can't control
_ _ _ _ _ _ _ _ _ _ _ _ _ _ _ _	_ _ _ _ _ _ _ _ _ _ _ _ _ _ _ _

'What can you do about it?'

'Don't worry too much about it.'

How big is my problem?   Examples

4. **Ginormous**: you need a lot of help from an adult.

_ _

3. **Big**: you can change it with some adult help.

_ _

2. **Medium**: you can change it with a little reminder.

_ _

1. **Little**: you can fix it all by yourself.

_ _

ABOUT THE AUTHOR

Niels is a father of two girls and lives with his wife in Melbourne, Australia. He is an author and mental toughness advocate. With his books, he hopes to make a positive difference, promote conversation, and help children learn about confidence, resilience, and a positive mindset.

Other books in the *My Strong Mind* series

ABOUT THE ILLUSTRATOR

Vanlaldiki is a digital artist and an illustrator from Mizoram, India. She fell in love with drawing when her dad drew his idea of their new home with colourful sketch-pens. She is a self-taught artist with 8 years experience and has worked with clients all over the world.

CPSIA information can be obtained
at www.ICGtesting.com
Printed in the USA
BVHW090813121121
621193BV00004B/320